"My dad won three trophies on the same day," Mike proudly told his dragon friends.

"Awesome!" said Sparkie.

"That's so knightly!" added Squirt.

"I bet I could win three trophies if we played knightly games!" Mike exclaimed.

"Why don't you set up some contests?" suggested the queen. "You can play for your dad's trophies."

"By the king's crown, that's it!" Mike declared. "I will try to win all three trophies and show everyone how knightly I am."

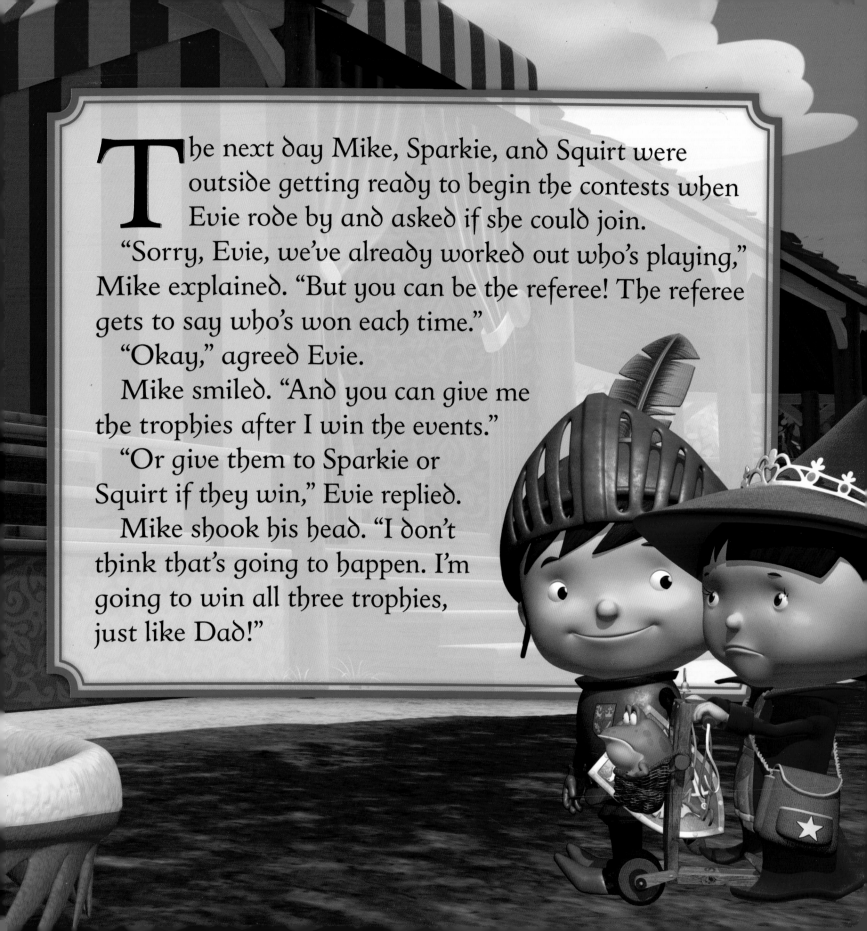

The next day Mike, Sparkie, and Squirt were outside getting ready to begin the contests when Evie rode by and asked if she could join.

"Sorry, Evie, we've already worked out who's playing," Mike explained. "But you can be the referee! The referee gets to say who's won each time."

"Okay," agreed Evie.

Mike smiled. "And you can give me the trophies after I win the events."

"Or give them to Sparkie or Squirt if they win," Evie replied.

Mike shook his head. "I don't think that's going to happen. I'm going to win all three trophies, just like Dad!"

The first knightly contest was to see who could run the fastest. Both Mike and Sparkie ran as fast as they could. It was a close race, but Sparkie finished just ahead of Mike. "Sparkie is the winner!" Evie cheered.

"Wait! . . . I don't think Sparkie really won," Mike replied. "He ran on four legs. And knights don't run on four legs, do they?"

Sparkie looked sad. "No, Mike. I suppose not," he said.

Evie didn't think this sounded very fair, and she told Mike that maybe they should run the race again. But Mike wasn't listening. Instead he took the trophy and headed over to the next contest.

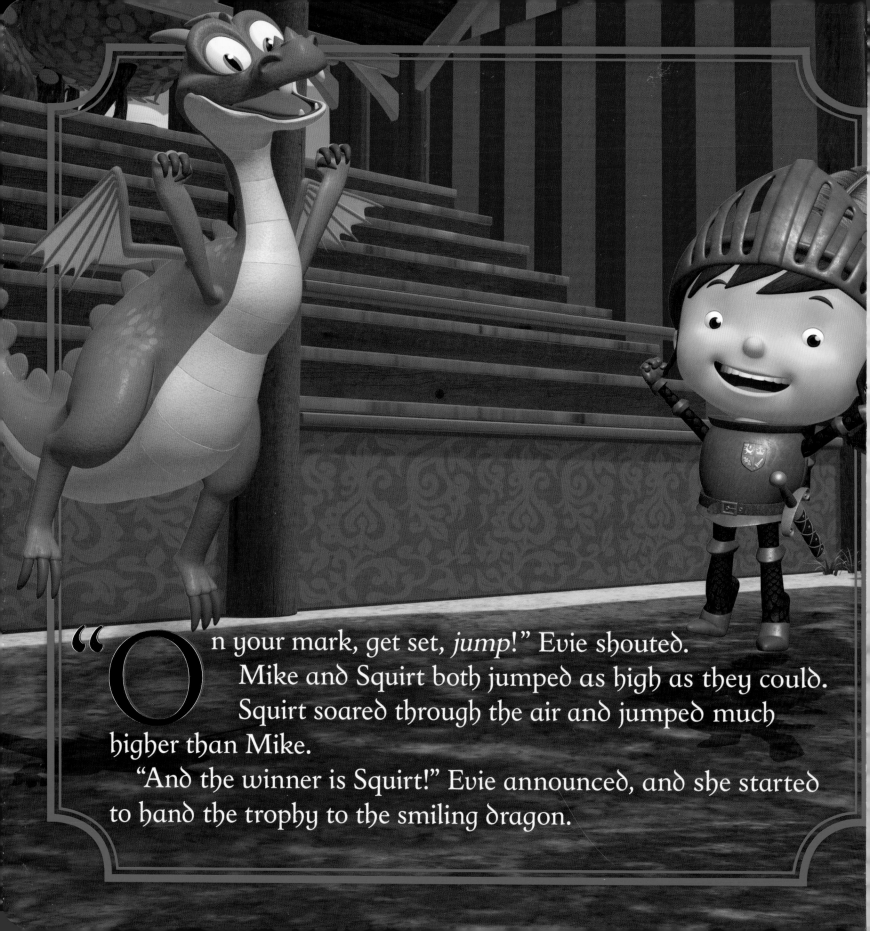

"On your mark, get set, *jump!*" Evie shouted.
 Mike and Squirt both jumped as high as they could.
 Squirt soared through the air and jumped much
higher than Mike.
 "And the winner is Squirt!" Evie announced, and she started
to hand the trophy to the smiling dragon.

But Mike stopped her. "Um, sorry, Squirt, but you're not the winner."
Evie was upset. "Why, Mike?"
"He wasn't jumping like a knight. Knights always wear a helmet," Mike explained. "And they carry a shield, but Squirt didn't. So I'm afraid Squirt loses," Mike said.
And with that, Mike took the second trophy from Evie.

Squirt tried not to look disappointed, but Evie was really mad. She told Mike she thought it was unfair to play that way.

But Mike wouldn't listen. He was already thinking about the next contest—the obstacle course.

Sparkie and Squirt arrived for the contest a few moments later, and Mike was surprised to see them dressed as knights with helmets and shields!

"Well . . . you do look very knightly!" Mike exclaimed.

"Thanks, Mike," said Squirt. "Evie helped us!"

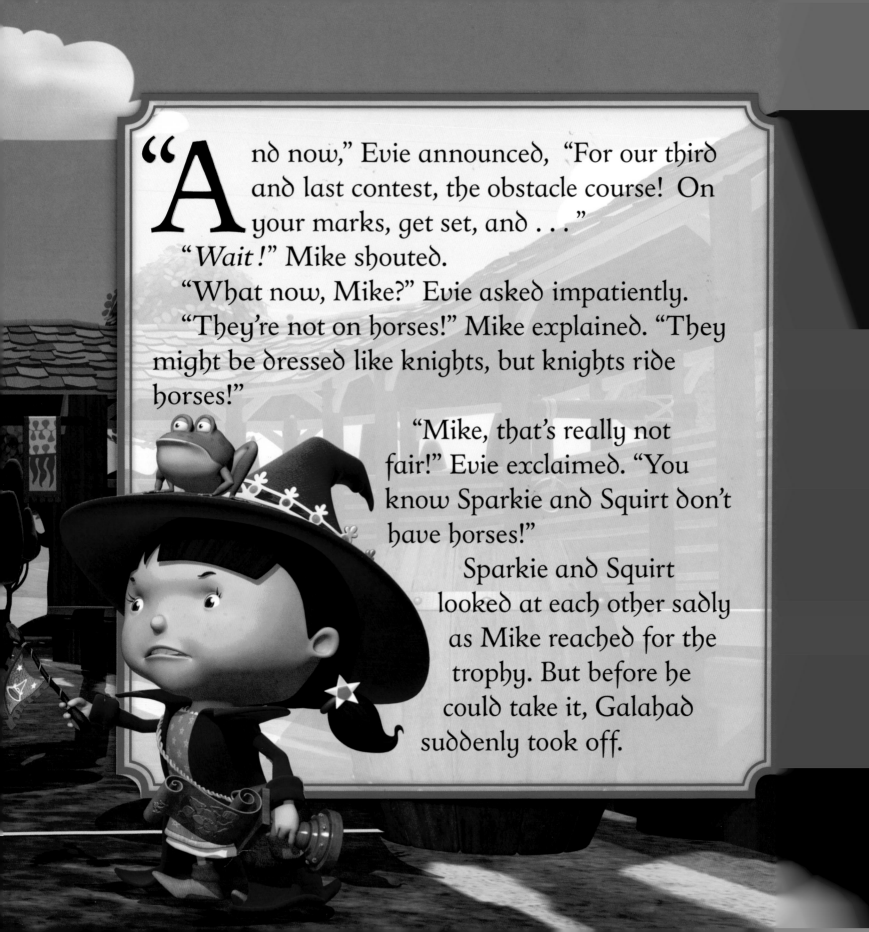

"And now," Evie announced, "For our third and last contest, the obstacle course! On your marks, get set, and . . ."

"*Wait!*" Mike shouted.

"What now, Mike?" Evie asked impatiently.

"They're not on horses!" Mike explained. "They might be dressed like knights, but knights ride horses!"

"Mike, that's really not fair!" Evie exclaimed. "You know Sparkie and Squirt don't have horses!"

Sparkie and Squirt looked at each other sadly as Mike reached for the trophy. But before he could take it, Galahad suddenly took off.

W hoa, Galahad!" Mike exclaimed. "What's wrong? I've already won the trophy."

But Galahad didn't look very happy about winning.

"Winning isn't as fun as I thought it would be," Mike said. "Not when everyone else is so sad."

"It's time to be a knight and do it right!" Mike shouted.

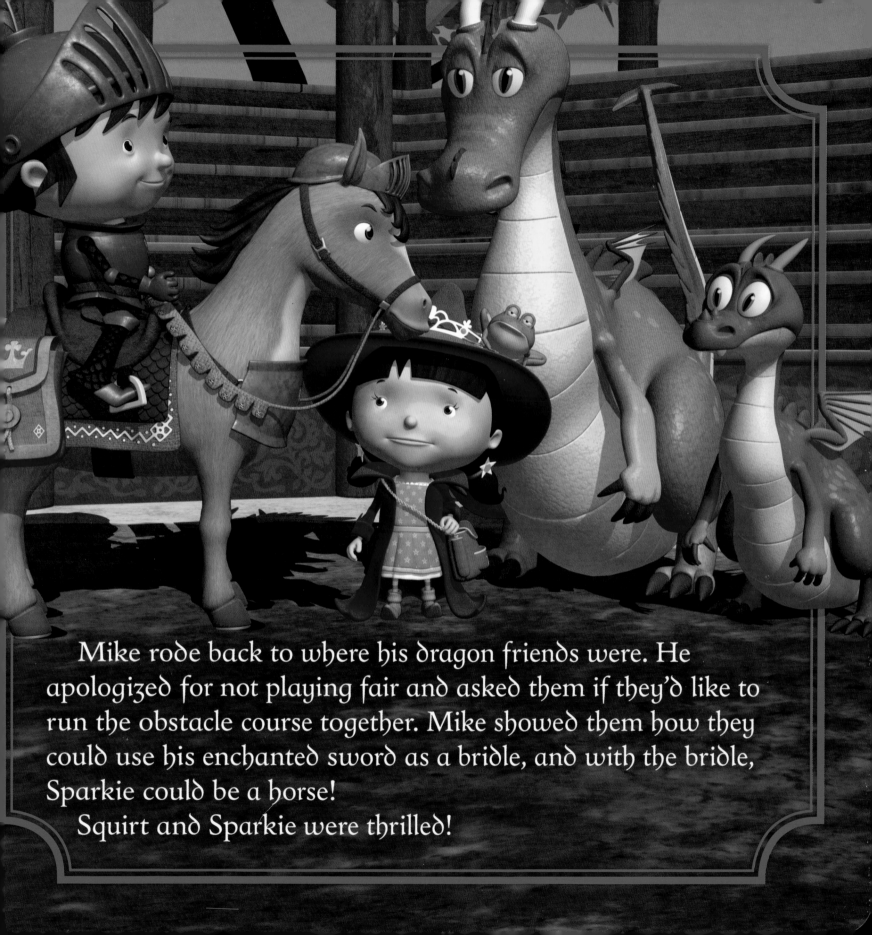

Mike rode back to where his dragon friends were. He apologized for not playing fair and asked them if they'd like to run the obstacle course together. Mike showed them how they could use his enchanted sword as a bridle, and with the bridle, Sparkie could be a horse!

Squirt and Sparkie were thrilled!

Evie walked over to the starting point. "Okay, is everybody ready? Now remember, Mike, play fair!"

"I'm going to, Evie," Mike answered. "So fair that you get to race too!"

And then Mike explained to Evie that it was her turn to be in one of the contests. She could ride Galahad! Mike loaned Evie his helmet, and he even offered to hold her wand for her while she rode.

Suddenly they heard a voice.

"Hello, everyone!"

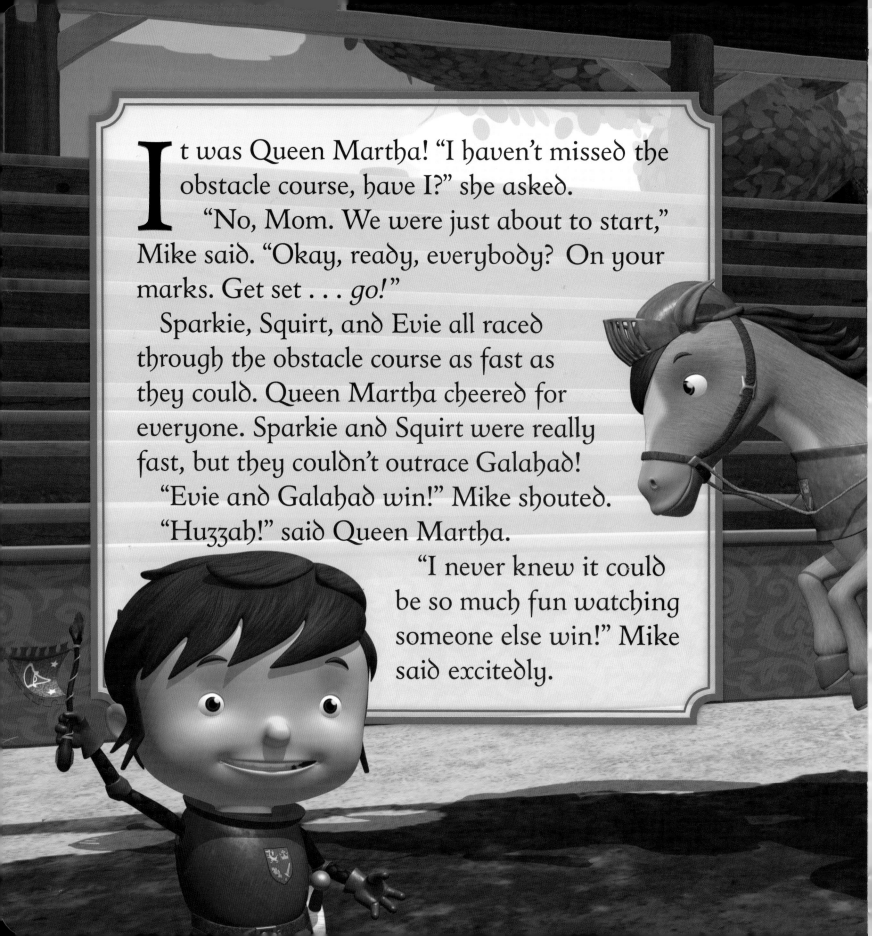

It was Queen Martha! "I haven't missed the obstacle course, have I?" she asked.

"No, Mom. We were just about to start," Mike said. "Okay, ready, everybody? On your marks. Get set . . . *go!*"

Sparkie, Squirt, and Evie all raced through the obstacle course as fast as they could. Queen Martha cheered for everyone. Sparkie and Squirt were really fast, but they couldn't outrace Galahad!

"Evie and Galahad win!" Mike shouted.

"Huzzah!" said Queen Martha.

"I never knew it could be so much fun watching someone else win!" Mike said excitedly.

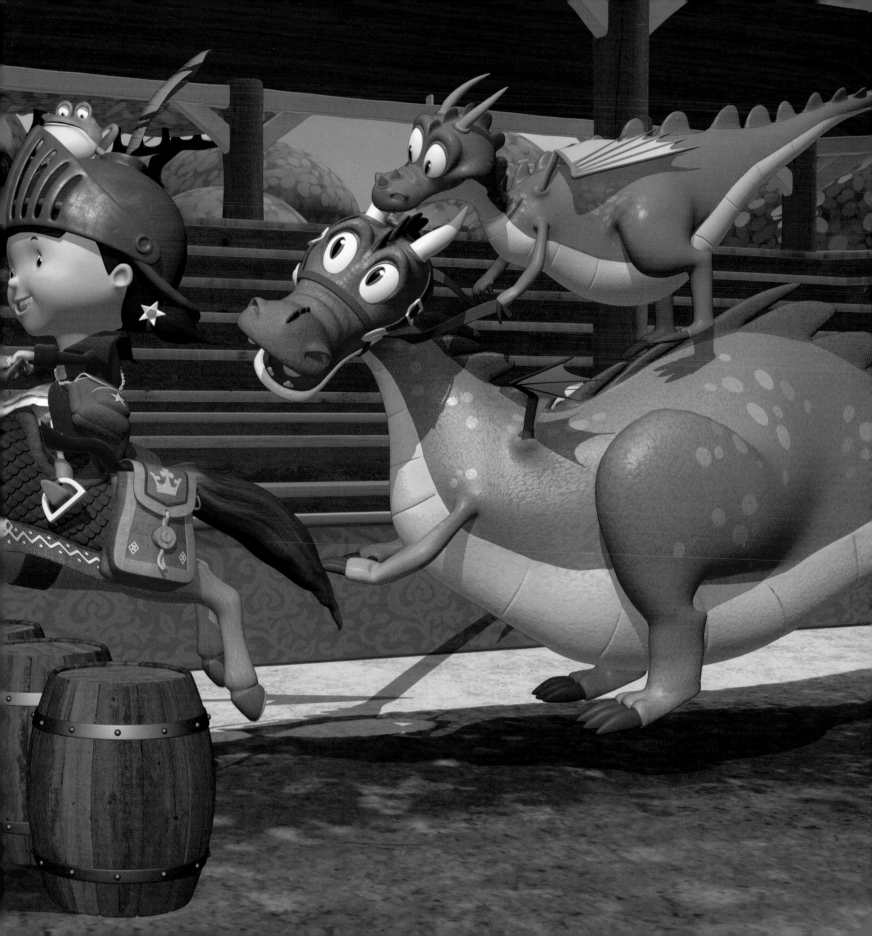

ike touched Evie's wand to the trophy table, and suddenly there were four trophies on the table, not three! But everyone was so excited they didn't notice.

Mike picked up the first trophy. "Sparkie definitely ran the fastest!" he said. And he handed the trophy to Sparkie.

"Whoopie!" said Evie.

Mike picked up the second trophy. "And Squirt definitely jumped the highest!" he said. And he handed the trophy to Squirt.

"Woo-hoo!" said Squirt.

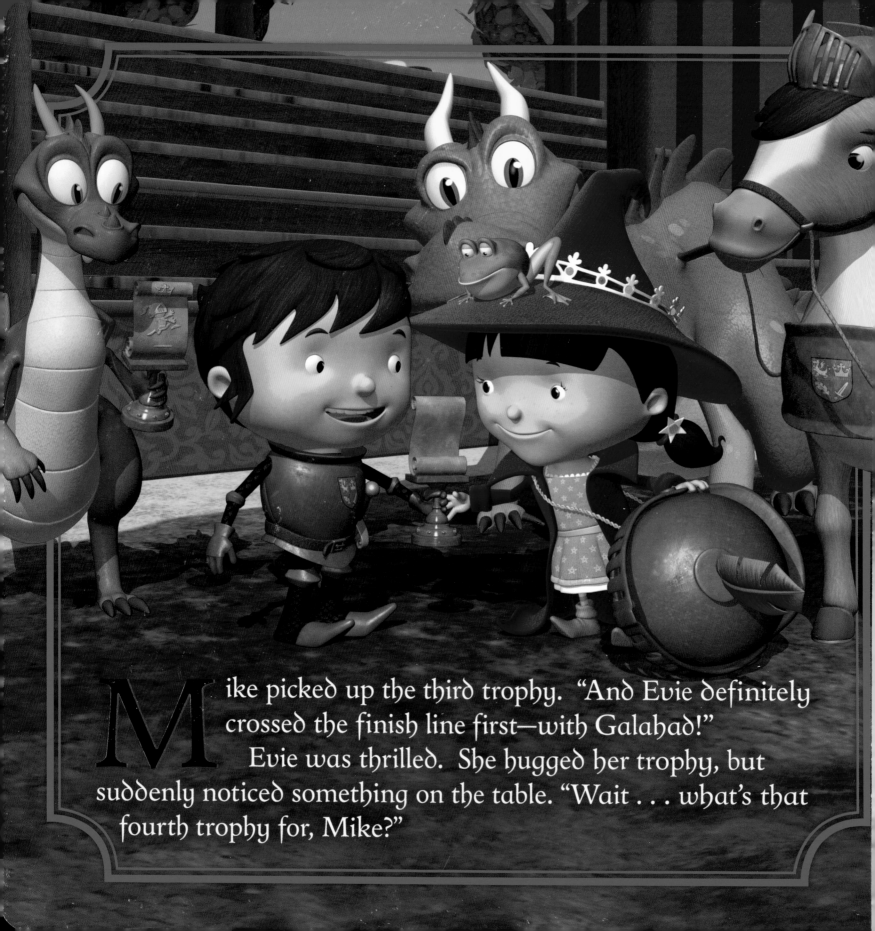

M ike picked up the third trophy. "And Evie definitely crossed the finish line first—with Galahad!"
Evie was thrilled. She hugged her trophy, but suddenly noticed something on the table. "Wait . . . what's that fourth trophy for, Mike?"